W9-DBQ-260

THE GOBLINS OF HAUBECK

"Hi! Look below. There goes Elsa, Our Baker's Daughter."

THE
GOBLINS OF HAUBECK

By

ALBERTA BANCROFT

Illustrated by
HAROLD SICHEL

NEW YORK
ROBERT M·McBRIDE & COMPANY
1925

COPYRIGHT, 1925, BY ALBERTA BANCROFT REID

PUBLISHED
AUGUST
1925

PRINTED IN THE UNITED STATES OF AMERICA

To
FRANCES ANN REID
and DONALD HUME FRY *Junior*
this book is
affectionately dedicated

Contents

Illustrations

THE GOBLINS OF HAUBECK

THE GOBLINS OF HAUBECK

T WAS NEAR SUNSET IN THE little city of Haubeck and all the little Goblins were hanging out of the mansard windows of the town, waiting for the stars.

Far below in the street people were walking to and fro. They looked up in the air and told one another that it was a fine day and that it would be a fine evening, but they said never a word about the little Goblins overhead. One might have thought that they did not know that the jolly little fellows were there at all.

All the while the Goblins were laughing and chattering as they leaned from the gable windows high

3

above the narrow street, or perched on the window
ledges, or hung from the wooden balconies where
the housewife had made her a bit of a garden, and
her thick crowded posies filled the air with sweetness.

Not a house in all Haubeck but had its Goblin—
three feet tall, four feet, maybe; slim, jolly, soft of
foot, and quick as the sunbeams dancing along the
wall—and the towers and church steeples held them
by the dozen.

They had lived in the little city for many years
now, greatly content with themselves and their sur-
roundings, harming no one and doing the people of
Haubeck much good. For it was not in their minds
to live in these people's houses, to walk in these people's streets and make no return for such happiness.
The houses must be kept in order, the roofs, yes, and
the streets too, after a manner.

They had a deal of talking to do this evening as
they waited for the stars, and they hailed one another from housetop to housetop and asked the company lolling in the belfries above to look out over
the city walls and tell what was going on without
there in the meadows and away towards the mountains behind the town.

"What shall we do to-night when once the stars are come?"

"We go to see the new shoes that Peter the Prentice makes," said some. "They will be ready for us, more than fifty of them, and we warrant you their fit will be better than ever before."

"We go to dance in the Town Hall," said others. "It will be gay, for the moon will light us. Hautchen, you must lead us," they added.

"Not I," said Hautchen sourly from a neighboring roof; and his little face drew itself into many wrinkles. "I have the stairs and the halls of my house to sweep to-night. Not one stroke of work does that fat woman do. All day long she sits in her chair by the doorstep with her hands folded in her lap—so. Or else she eats coffee cake. That is what it is to have strange people come into one's house." He settled himself crossly on the window ledge. "Is one to go on slaving forever for such a lot? And they have not even the politeness to set out a little cake and a saucer of milk for me."

Sympathetic, shaggy little heads were shaken from all the houses round about.

"The New Baker is no gentleman," the Goblins

declared. "And his Fat Wife is even worse. You must speak to Lurin about it."

"But Lurin is not here," objected Hautchen. "And who knows where his wanderlegs have taken him or how long they will keep him away?"

The little heads were nodded again. Lurin was without doubt the wisest Goblin in all Haubeck. The only trouble with him was that he was not content to live quietly in the town, properly as a Goblin should, but was forever going off nobody knew where into the big country round about and staying for months at a time. He never would settle down and take a house and look to the needs of the family who lived in it, which was clearly the whole duty of Goblins; but always made for one of the belfries when he came back to Haubeck and lodged there with the gay fellows who had no household responsibilities upon their shoulders—there were not houses enough in Haubeck to go around in those days—and the belfry dwellers were made happy by his presence. But the House Goblins scolded and said that it was no way to live. Why, they would have given him the Town Hall if he would only have taken it.

So the little heads nodded when he told his troubles and the Goblins all agreed that it was not right. It was not right that he should have so much work to do. It was not right that Haubeck should have such lazy people living in it as the Fat Wife of the New Baker, who had come to town not so long since with a whitewashed wooden wedding cake which he kept in his show window. It was not right. Lurin was the only one who could help in a case like that. And Lurin surely would help—if he were only there to hear about it.

The sun went down as they talked it over, and the purple haze began to rise and the swallows wheeled their last in the upper golden light. And they none of them spoke till they were hailed by another batch of Goblins farther down the roofs. These were craning down into the street and pointing.

"Hi!" they called out. "Hi! Look below. There goes Elsa, Our Baker's Daughter."

All leaned over to see. They had taken to calling the Old Baker, the one who had always lived in Haubeck, "Our Baker" since the New Baker with the Fat Wife had come to town.

Hautchen leaned over with the rest. His heart was like to burst. It was not that he grudged Nickel his position—Nickel was the Old Baker's House Goblin—but, oh, dear, some folk had all the luck.

"She grows prettier every day," the Goblins declared, still looking. "A wonder is Lurin can bear to stay away at all, when he could look at her if he were here."

Lurin had cared for Elsa years ago when she was a little, little girl and her mother died and there was no one to make her happy—that was before the Goblins left Oberon's Country and came to live in Haubeck—and there was no one on earth whom he loved better.

"It is enough to have one baker in Haubeck," the Goblins added gloomily. "The other one need not have come at all."

The Baker's Daughter tripped along below them with never a look above. But the little Goblins smiled down and kissed their hands to her.

She had hardly passed before cries and clangings arose in the evening air and the sound of many voices. The big, iron Town Gate which had been closed for the night swung wearily open, and there was more noise and there were more voices before it was safely shut again.

Then with a bump and a clatter the Tin Smith's cart came up the street, with the Tin Smith seated in front, red of face and broad of smile, because he was home again after his long journey and had not had to camp till morning in the meadow outside the Town Wall.

With screams of joy the Tin Smith's wife and children ran out to meet him. The neighbors crowded up to shake him by the hand and the tin pans—there were only one or two left—bounced merrily up and down in the back of the covered wagon.

But none of the people saw what the Goblins overhead saw—how two slim legs slid out from between the back flaps of that covered wagon, and a little fellow with a slim body and a shaggy head slipped into the Tin Smith's house and raced for the attic stairs.

That was Bibel, the Tin Smith's Goblin.

Bibel always went with the Tin Smith when the Tin Smith took to the road. Bibel saw to it that the tin pans did not leap out of the wagon and that the pennies that were paid for them were not lost in any crack. And he kept the old horse from running the wagon into the ditch—the Tin Smith was not much of a driver, but the Tin Smith did not know that—and he mended the worn harness o' nights when other people were asleep. The Tin Smith would never have been able to get along without Bibel—but the Tin Smith did not know that. He did not know anything about Bibel.

Bibel had a twin brother called Rig; and Rig stayed at home in Haubeck and looked after the Tin Smith's family.

Bibel now made for the attic and climbed out of the mansard window and settled himself on the window ledge beside his brother Rig. And all the Goblins round about shouted their "Welcome Home" to him across the roofs.

If Bibel had come half an hour later he would not have found a one of them there—they would have been scattered to all the ends of the town and the business of the night would have been begun. As it was, they put off this beginning, so as to have a few words with Bibel before starting out. But there were so many Goblins and most of the roofs were so far away from the Tin Smith's that the little Folk ended by betaking themselves to Lurin's belfry. And there they spent half the night, crowded together gossiping beneath the great bronze bells.

Bibel had had a splendid time traveling with the Tin Smith about the country. They had journeyed far and he had seen new places. They had made more money than ever before. They had many orders for new pots— But Bibel wanted to know all the news of the town. How was the Baker's Daughter?

Pretty as a ripe cherry, and as sweet. All the young men of Haubeck were making eyes at her.

Bibel laughed. He could tell a tale. There were young men outside of Haubeck too, whose eyes and thoughts had a way of wandering off after the Baker's Daughter. There was the young Miller of Brocken, for instance—well, he would tell them about that some time. At present he must hear the town news. How was the New Baker? And his Fat Wife?

The Goblins looked solemn. Worse than ever. Worse than ever, they said. Hautchen was having a dreadful time of it. He could not stand it much longer. If Lurin did not come home pretty soon and help straighten things out—

But Bibel shook his head. Lurin had lost his Sleep Cap, he told them, and was searching for it the country over.

The Goblins groaned. There was great fright

among them, for they knew what that meant. The worst thing that can happen to a Goblin is to lose his Sleep Cap. Once lost, he cannot go to sleep in the winter-time until he finds it. Lurin would have much trouble. There was no telling how long it would take him to find his cap. They were more sorry than they could say. That was what came of journeying into the wide country, they said. Goblins were meant to stay properly at home.

Yes; that was true, agreed Bibel—unless it was business that took them abroad, as was the case with him.

Here Hautchen, who had slipped over to the belfry for a while, in spite of all the work he had to do that night, nearly wept. He had been trying to tell Bibel of the wickedness of the New Baker's Fat Wife—to sit with her hands in her lap all the day. It was a crime. But Bibel was not paying much attention to him.

Bibel was too busy talking about the young Miller of Brocken and his Mill. The Tin Smith had stopped at the Mill on the Brocken for five days. It was because a new oven had to be set up at the Mill. And Bibel had put in his time watching the young Miller.

When the young Miller was not working like a

beaver, he lay beside the stream, where the big, green millwheel turned and the water rushed over the dam, and sighed and made verses and called the name of Elsa the Baker's Daughter of Haubeck. And if he did not do that, he took his ass and a sack of flour and started off in the early morning—and he did not come home again until the night. And no one at the Mill knew where he went.

The Goblins laughed. They knew well enough where the Miller spent his time. He and the ass and the sack of flour came to Haubeck. And the young man had much ado in getting through the street where the old bake-shop stood and Elsa the Baker's Daughter could be seen at her work within.

"She likes him well," the Goblins told Bibel. "She likes him better than any of the young men of Haubeck. It is as plain to see as the nose on the Weaver's face. The young Miller will not spend much more time lying beside the stream bank and speaking her name—he will have better things to do."

But Hautchen, who had been sitting in a corner of the belfry, hugging his knees and counting all the work he had to do before morning, had been thinking. And now, as he unwound himself and stood up ready to leave, he asked, "If a trouble should come to the Baker's Daughter, do you think Lurin would come back to Haubeck to help her—even though his Sleep Cap had not been found?"

And the Goblins pondered over the question and then said that they thought he would.

WHAT HAUTCHEN DID

WHAT HAUTCHEN DID

HAUTCHEN WENT BACK TO HIS
house. He had much thinking to do.
And yet, he assured himself, there was
really no need to do any thinking at
all, for had not all the Goblins of
Haubeck said the same thing? That Elsa liked the
young Miller of Brocken better than any of the young
men of Haubeck? And that, if any trouble should

17

come to her, Lurin would surely know it and come back to help her?

Well, then, the matter was quite simple. All Hautchen had to do was to begin.

But in spite of knowing this, it took Hautchen four whole days and nights to screw up his courage to the beginning point.

Then he set to work.

It was less than a week before the Goblins were telling one another that their Baker's Daughter was not looking so bright as usual. And it was less than two weeks before they were shaking their heads and saying that something was quite, quite wrong. And it did not need Nickel to tell them so either—Nickel had found her in tears in the daytime and heard her sobbing at night—for all one had to do was to look at her.   . .

And was it not strange that the young Miller of Brocken did not seem to be speaking with her any more—even if he did come to town so often as usual with his donkey and his sack of flour? And he looked so—so different—when he did come.

It was the week after that that one of the Goblins was sure he had seen Lurin slipping along one of the streets of Haubeck. And the same evening another was sure that he had seen Lurin too. But each time Lurin disappeared—in a twinkling—without speaking. So how could they be quite sure?

And the day after that the Baker's Daughter was lost.

Not just a little "I stepped out to visit one of the neighbors and did not leave word where I was going" lost. Not that kind of a lost at all. But a real lost, that lasted half of the morning and all of the afternoon and far into the night.

All of Haubeck was stirred by it. The little city had been searched through by three o'clock; and by four most of the people were streaming out of the town to search for Elsa in the meadows and mountains beyond the Town Wall.

Most of the Goblins had gathered in the belfries to wait for news. And there along towards midnight Rig, the Tin Smith's stay-at-home Goblin, burst in upon them with word that Elsa was found again—she had hurt her foot while looking for watercress in a little gorge among the hills and had not been able to walk back to Haubeck. But she could walk again now and was back again. And her father the Old Baker was with her and so was the young Miller of Brocken. And she looked quite as blooming as usual—perhaps more blooming even. And Lurin really had been in Haubeck and was even now on his way to the belfries to greet them.

Hard upon Rig came Lurin. And after Lurin came Nickel, the Old Baker's House Goblin, very stiff and sour and looking as though he had to do three bakings in one night. And behind Nickel every Goblin in Haubeck piled into the belfry. Last of all came Hautchen, his eyes large as a cat's by night and his hair on end with excitement.

Lurin did not seem the same Lurin at all. His smile was gone and his mouth was a straight line turning down grimly at the corners. He did not speak until he caught sight of Hautchen squeezing into the belfry; and then he pointed a finger quite dreadfully at Hautchen with his arm out straight and snapped, "You ought to be thrown out of the window."

All the other Goblins held their breath to listen.

"But if you would only listen," begged Hautchen. "The New Baker's Fat Wife— The wickedness of that woman—"

"It is all one to me," snapped Lurin. "When a man

is House Goblin, he cannot expect to sit and hold his hands. The work is part of the honor. You have made more trouble and unhappiness—"

"Not I," declared Hautchen stoutly. "I could not have done better. You see for yourself how happy they are."

"What did he do? What did he do?" went the whisper round the belfry, as the Goblins looked at one another, wondering what the trouble was.

"But what business has Hautchen to come meddling into my house?" asked Nickel, the Old Baker's House Goblin, angrily. Nickel was young and hot-headed and thought the Baker's Daughter the most wonderful person in the world. "Do I go prying into the house of the New Baker? I do not. I stay where I belong. Why does Hautchen not stay where he belongs? I can look after my house without any help from him."

"What did he do? What did he do?" the Goblins asked again.

But this time they asked Lurin and Nickel instead of asking one another. And it was Lurin who answered them.

"I will tell you what he did," said Lurin furiously. "I knew something was wrong. Over many hills and

valleys where I was hunting for my Sleep Cap I felt
of a sudden that things were not going well with Elsa,
Our Baker's Daughter in Haubeck; that she was in
trouble and needed me. So I came home to help her.
Three days I have been in Haubeck, trying to learn
what that trouble was. To-day I learn what the trouble was—and who caused it." And he glared at
Hautchen. "Listen to what I heard when I came upon
Elsa and the young Miller of Brocken in the gorge
where she hurt her foot and where he found her, before the others, when all Haubeck was hunting for
her. Listen. Coming upon them—for of course I was
hunting too—I heard him say, 'You have made me
very unhappy.'

"And she said, 'I have not done anything.'

" 'You have frightened me to death,' he said.

" 'I went to hunt watercress,' she said.

" 'You have treated me very badly,' he told her.
'You will now tell me why.' And then he said—listen well, all of you—he said—and he was angry—
'It was Wednesday, two weeks gone yesterday. That
was the start. In the afternoon I chanced to be coming
down your street. You were sitting in your window.
I greeted you. You jumped up, never so much as nod-

"*I heard him say, 'You have made me very unhappy.'*"

ding your head to me, and ran away from the window
—and did not come back.'

"And then the Baker's Daughter cried out, 'But I
did not see you. Wednesday, two weeks gone, you say?
I remember. I was at the window and there was a
great noise in the pantry. I ran to see. The cat had
tipped over a pan of milk. It took me one whole hour
to make all clean again. And Friday the next week
the same thing happened—'

"And the Miller broke in, all breathless, 'When you
were sitting on the step outside the bakeshop?'

"And she answered, 'Two whole pans of cream.
All over the floor. I beat her well, I promise you. It
took me well-nigh the whole afternoon to make all
clean again. But how did you know that I was on the
step?'

" 'I was coming down the street,' said the Miller.
'You ran into the house. But I thought that I would
follow and learn why you should run away when I
came to see you—'

" 'But I did not run away,' cried the Baker's
Daughter.

" 'And then when I tried to enter the bakeshop—
the door was locked,' he said. He was very angry.

"And then our Elsa began to cry. 'I do not understand it,' she sobbed. 'I did not lock the door. Why should I lock the door of my father's bakeshop before the night? People might want to come to buy!'

"And then he said, 'But how about Monday? Did the cat spill the cream on the pantry floor on Monday too?'

"And the Baker's Daughter said, 'I do not know. I was not at home. Early in the morning the Weaver came and said his wife was ailing and would I go and stay with her. I was with her all the day.'

"Then the Miller of Brocken looked like one wildered and he said, 'It passes my understanding. Then who did it? I chanced to have business in Haubeck on Monday too. And I chanced to pick some flowers and brought them to you. No one was in the shop and I laid them on your little table there. I went out again. But hardly was I in the street when my flowers came flying out of the door after me. They hit me on the head and knocked my hat off. I thought you did it.'

"That is what the young Miller of Brocken said to Elsa," said Lurin solemnly. "And—"

"And I saw Hautchen come into my bakeshop—my bakeshop, mind you," broke in Nickel, breathing heavily. "I saw him seize that bunch of flowers the Miller left for our Elsa and throw it at his head. It knocked his hat off. I would have had dealings with Hautchen then. But Lurin seized me—until that moment I did not know that Lurin was in Haubeck—and said I should do nothing until he learned all the trouble with our Elsa. Our Elsa's trouble was that Hautchen there."

Then Nickel stopped and glared at Hautchen. And Lurin glared at Hautchen. And all the little Goblins lined about the walls in the belfry stared and gasped and stared again at Hautchen.

And Hautchen, standing up in the midst of them with his eyes large as a cat's by night and his hair on end with excitement, drew a deep breath and said, "Well, yes, then. I did it. I threw the bunch of flowers at the head of the Miller of Brocken. And I locked the bakeshop door so that he could not get in. And I upset the pans of cream—both times. And the young Miller of Brocken has asked Our Baker for Elsa in marriage and everybody is happy. And if I had not done as I did, the young Miller would not have asked for Elsa for months to come. So you see how I have helped the Baker's Daughter."

"You did not tip the cream over so as to help the Baker's Daughter," Nickel cried hotly. "And that is not the reason you threw the flowers at the head of the young Miller of Brocken either."

He could not get over the insult of another Goblin's having dared to come into his house—while he was up in the attic chasing mice with the cat—and make trouble for his mistress.

"You wanted to make the Baker's Daughter unhappy, because you knew that if you did Lurin would come back to help her, and then you could get him to help you in the matter of the New Baker's Fat Wife—"

"Is that true?" Lurin asked in an awful voice.

And Hautchen broke down and began to weep.

"If you only knew what I have gone through," he sobbed. "That terrible woman. Now she will no longer make the beds of a morning. And in the afternoon when all the Goblins of Haubeck do as they please, I have to set the table for coffee—and even have to clear it off again. It is enough to drive one mad. What am I to do?"

But Lurin's face was as red as fire and he was jumping up and down in his anger.

"Talk not to me," he cried. "I will not help you. You are more than worthless. All this need not have happened if it had not been for you."

Hautchen tried to say something about the New Baker's Fat—

But Lurin turned an enraged back.

"I will hear nothing of the New Baker's Fat Wife," he declared. "I shall go out into the country again to look for my Sleep Cap."

And that is what he did.

And Hautchen stayed behind and had a miserable time of it. The other Goblins would have nothing to do with him. And the New Baker's Fat Wife grew worse and worse. And surely no one would have thought that possible.

Hautchen thought about his trouble until he feared his head would drop off from the pain in it. And then he made up his mind.

"Every one thinks me as bad as can be," he said to himself, as he tried to rock the screaming baby in the cradle to sleep. "And Lurin will not tell me what to do. So it were as well to be bad and have some comfort from it."

Then trouble began. For Hautchen did a dreadful

thing—a thing which would have made the hair to rise on the heads of all the Goblins in Haubeck, if they had only known about it.

The next morning there was no breakfast for the New Baker when he came into the kitchen to get it, and the New Baker's Fat Wife was waddling around with a face as cross as two sticks, fussing among the pots and dishes, trying to find out where things were kept. When he asked her what was the matter, she said she had the toothache. She had never told him that there was an unseen Somebody in the house they had come to live in in Haubeck that did all the work—if only one refused to do any work one's self.

That day the beds were not made in the house of the New Baker. The halls were not swept; nor the stairs. And no room was set to rights. When the Fat Wife started the fire for dinner, it was blown out six times running. And when at last a merry blaze was going and a dinner of sorts on the way, the kettle took to dumping hot water on to the Fat Wife whenever she came near the stove. The potatoes jumped down into the ashes. And the soup pot overset on the floor.

That was the first day.

The New Baker was an angry man, for he was used
to having his house affairs run smoothly. The New
Baker's Fat Wife was angry too. She had good reason.
And the New Baker's children spent most of the time
slapping one another, or crying and saying that there
was no one for them to play with.

The second day things went even worse. For all
these things happened again in the house. And in the
bakeshop—well, the New Baker said he could not
understand it. Whenever a body opened the street-
door, a loaf of bread or a cake or a shower of pretzels
went flying at his head. Children were hit in the face
and went screaming home to tell what the New Baker
had done to them. Angry women made their escape
from the shop and called back that the New Baker
would see whether respectable women could be in-
sulted in that way. Some half-grown boys thought that
it would be a good time to throw rocks at the whitewashed wooden wedding cake through the glass—and
did it. And the New Baker had three fights with the
men who came to find out what he meant by throw-
ing things at their wives and children and were treated
in the same way.

The New Baker said that his hair would turn white

if things did not change. The Fat Wife cried all the
time. So did the children.

At the end of a week the New Baker said that it
was no use—the house was bewitched. The people of
Haubeck would not believe it. They would have nothing more to do with them. The family would have to
move to another town.

He spent most of his time in trying to mend the
broken whitewashed wedding cake and his Fat Wife
had to do all the packing. The children made as much
trouble as they knew how to make. They were still
complaining that there was no one to play with them
any more.

The day they left Haubeck Hautchen went up into
the attic and wept for joy. He could have told how
all those things came to pass in the house of the New
Baker—who was now gone away. Only no one asked
him.

Nevertheless, it was the happiest day of his life.

HINZELMANN

HINZELMANN

HE BAKER'S DAUGHTER AND the young Miller of Brocken were married.

All the Haubeckers followed the young couple to the church to see the ceremony and afterwards went out to the Mill, where the festivities were continued after they were finished at the Baker's house at Haubeck.

And there was not a Goblin in all Haubeck, house Goblin or belfry Goblin, who did not go out to the Mill to watch the doings of the mortal people in whose houses they lived.

There had been a great deal of talking among them before they found a way of managing this. They wanted to see Elsa married. And they wanted to reach the Mill before all the excitement was over. And it was sad but true that they were a small Folk with legs that could not always keep up with horses, and sometimes not even with donkeys. They ended by hanging on in great numbers to every wagon that left the town. And the result was that the horses were slow and the drivers were angry and the Goblins on foot were able to keep up and changed places with their fellows on the wagons before the journey was over.

Hautchen was happier than he had ever been in his life. To have seen Elsa married, to have driven to the Mill in the very wagon with her—that was much. But to have Lurin come up, swing an arm over his shoulder and ask if he did not think that the bride's veil was vastly fine and became her vastly well—that was almost more than a Goblin heart could keep on beating under.

Lurin had forgotten all about Hautchen's ungoblin-like behavior of the past spring. It was as though Hautchen had never spilt milk in another Goblin's house, or thrown flowers at the young Miller's head and brought trouble to the Baker's Daughter. He was so happy that he beamed on everybody. He even took Hautchen over the Mill and explained to him what a worthy place it was and how comfortably mortal people could live there.

Hautchen thought about it as he trudged home with the other Goblins. As I said, he was happier than he had ever been in all his life before. He had had a perfect day. He was going to have more perfect days in the future. The Goblins came to him, one and all, and told him he was a fine fellow. They patted him on the back, and one or two even whispered that it was a clever thing to have done to have thrown the flowers at the head of the young Miller. The flowers having struck the head, set the head a-thinking— Oh, it was a wonderful thing to have done.

Besides this, Hautchen was happy for quite another reason.

For the past week men had come to his empty house, where no one had lived since the New Baker and his Fat Wife and their children moved away. They had come with clank of boot and key, had opened, prowled about, cleared their throats, grunted, wriggled the door handles and window fastenings and raised their hands to heaven—the one declaring the place a dog kennel where one could expect nothing better than to find one's grave; the other protesting that any young housewife would weep for joy at the very thought of being able to live in so beautiful a home. Yesterday, Hautchen gathered from the grunts that passed between them, that the matter had been settled. Some one was coming to make a home in his house again.

The Goblins ended the night with a dance in the Town Hall. And when in the early morning Hautchen made for his own bleak dwelling-place where there was no furniture and everything was bare—oh! oh! the family had moved in.

He tiptoed about in the slanting sunlight, going from room to room. There was a fresh young housewife already bustling about. Her cheeks were like apples with dimples in them. Her eyes were like twinkling stars. It made one's mouth water to see the way she handled her pots and pans.

Hautchen beamed upon her from behind a door. He told himself that her pans should be brighter than ever before. Her kitchen floor—oh, he would scrub it three times a week. He hugged himself as he thought of the pleasure of helping such a woman with her work.

There was a good looking young husband, thumping and bumping boxes, putting pieces of furniture together and whistling at the top of his lungs. Hautchen decided that it would be a pleasure to clean the hall floor after his muddy boots.

And then he went to have a look at the children.

Three children—oh, and one of them a baby! He looked into the cradle—yes, it was a beautiful baby. It opened its eyes and laughed at him as he looked down upon it. And the other two children were so different from the children of the New Baker's Fat Wife.

Truly, Hautchen had come upon pleasant days.

He spent near on a week helping the family unpack. The husband and wife smiled upon one another continually. They kept telling one another that the settling down had never been so easy before, or the children so good while it was going on. Hautchen was proud indeed. He pulled at ropes harder than ever and spent every spare moment amusing the children.

At last, on the fifth evening, husband and wife put their arms around each other and laughed and cried and whispered, "It must be true. It must be true. At last we are rid of him."

Hautchen wiped his eyes in sympathy and wondered what it was all about. He went off to the belfries to brag about the family that had come to live with him.

But he had not half finished with what he had to say when he remembered that the woman had said that she must churn on the morrow—and the churn had not been scalded since it had been unpacked.

So he slid down from the belfry and hurried back to his kitchen and rolled the churn out of its corner.

The churn was strangely heavy. Hautchen stopped to catch his breath, and, as he did so, the dasher rose solemnly up in air. The cover rose after it. A black cap and black hair and a dark little face with a pair of sharp little eyes followed.

"What ails you to be rolling this churn around at the dead of night? Have you lost your wits?" a sulky little voice asked shortly.

But Hautchen had been made bold by happiness. He pushed the churn over and in doing so tipped a small man onto the floor.

"What do you mean," he asked stiffly, "by hiding

The newcomer . . . laughed and laughed.

yourself in my mistress's churn? And what is your name? And what are you doing in our house?"

The newcomer picked himself up and picked up the dasher and pointed it at Hautchen and laughed and laughed. Hautchen felt his eyes begin to burn and he swallowed hard. He had become much too important these days to take a laugh from any one—least of all from a stranger who hid in other people's churns. And now this person was even mimicking him.

"Your mistress. Your mistress!" The horrid little man dropped the dasher to hold his sides. "Ho, ho! And your mistress's churn! And 'our house,' is it? And you wish to know my name. Well, Spindle Legs, my name is Hinzelmann. And I am here, because I go wherever goes the woman whom you are free enough to call your mistress. And let me tell you this, Spindle Legs— What have you done to your mouth? It looks as though it did not know the way to turn up—let me tell you this: I have but to raise my little finger; I have but to make one little sound so that they can hear; I have but to whisk past the open door, so that they can see—and straightway there will be a wild commotion, in 'our house.' The things which you have been help-ing to unpack so carefully while I sat at ease in the churn will be bundled into their boxes again and the whole family will trundle off to try to find a new home."

The speaker began to laugh anew.

There seemed much likelihood of a fight. Hautchen felt himself bristling all over.

But then, Hautchen was even more curious than he was angry. And this Hinzelmann did not laugh when he talked. And just at present he seemed to want to talk more than he did anything else. And he ended by perching himself on the kitchen table and with that objectionable dasher in his hand he told Hautchen a long story.

His name was Hinzelmann—as he said before. While he was a small and young person, his father sold him to a farmer for a round, red cheese. His father was an Elf of some sort who was known throughout the land as a thriftless fellow with a fondness for all kinds of mortal food.

Hinzelmann, then, was sold. And he could no more get rid of the farmer than the farmer could get rid of him.

They both had unpleasant times. But Hinzelmann thought that on the whole he had the better of it. If he was ordered to do the work which he hated—well, one could be invisible at will. And what was the farmer to do when he could see nobody? If the farmer's wife threw hot water on him when he ran round and round the table instead of setting it as he had been told—why, others too could tip water out of pots, upset milk in the pantry, crumble cake on the storeroom floor and throw potatoes from the dark behind the cellar door. It was no wish of his to have been sold, said Hinzelmann. He had no wish to belong to a family and be handed down like a stick of furniture from one to another. But still, the life had its compensations—and he told Hautchen the story of the potatoes all over again.

The farmer had tried to get rid of Hinzelmann. But the thing was not so easy. A mortal, having bought one of elfin kind, can sell him, yes, if any one will buy. But no one would buy Hinzelmann. A mortal can give away an Elf—but the one who is to receive the Elf must know it. And no one would have Hinzelmann as a gift.

There seemed to be but one way of parting company from Hinzelmann and this, at last, the farmer did. He died. And he left Hinzelmann in a written will, which the village scribe drew up, to a maiden sister of his whom he particularly hated.

Hinzelmann betook himself to his new home— much against the will of the owner—and continued to give trouble. He told Hautchen the things he did and Hautchen's hair stood on end with horror.

After some years the old lady also died and Hinzelmann again changed hands.

The old lady had had a grand-niece living with her. She sometimes seemed a little fond of the girl. But the niece ran away and married a young man whom the aunt did not like—a carver of wood and a builder of chimneys he was—and when the girl came back to explain that she really could not have done otherwise, because she did not like the old man whom her aunt had picked out for her, why she was ordered off the place and the dogs were set on her.

This young woman, the wife of the good looking young Wood Carver, was Hinzelmann's present mistress. The aunt had bequeathed him to her in a fit of rage when she was on her deathbed—and Hinzelmann had cheerfully betaken himself to his next home and proceeded to make himself as unwelcome there as he had been in the others.

Indeed, so great a plague had he become—Hinzelmann told these things himself and seemed quite proud of them—that the family had already moved three times in the hope of getting rid of him. But Hinzelmann was not to be got rid of. This last time, though, he had hidden himself in the churn and was keeping very quiet so as to make them think that he was really lost at last—and then they would be all the more unhappy when they found out that he was still there, ready to make all the mischief that lay in his power.

Hinzelmann kissed his hand as he finished his tale and asked Hautchen to give an account of his doings. But Hautchen was all for asking questions.

"What will they do when they find out that you are still here with them?" he said.

"They will pick up and pack up and leave the town," Hinzelmann answered comfortably.

Hautchen could have wrung his hands and wept he was so unhappy at the thought of such a possibility. But he thought quickly and he talked to himself under his breath while he was asking another question or two. And then when Hinzelmann repeated his own question, Hautchen gave him such a tale of the beautiful city of Haubeck, of the wonders to be seen there, the joyous life to lead, the Goblins, their wondrous doings and the wondrous Folk they knew—that Hinzelmann listened at last with his mouth open and his eyes bulging.

"These things I must see," he gasped. "It would be more than sad, if my family should up and leave. I will be very quiet. I will not so much as spill a pan of cream or pinch one of the children. Then they will not know that I am here. They will stay here and all will be well."

He put the dasher back into the churn and rolled the churn back into its corner. And Hautchen sat down and mopped his brow. He could have jumped for joy. He had gained what he wanted.

THE WITCH CLOAK

THE WITCH CLOAK

"HOW LONG HAVE YOU LIVED in Haubeck?" asked Hinzelmann of Haubeck.

Hautchen was mopping the kitchen floor. Hinzelmann was sitting on the kitchen table. The stars were blinking against the windows.

"I have lived here so long that I have nearly forgotten when I came," answered Hautchen, as he mopped away. "When I think about it, it seems as though it must be a dream that I ever lived in Oberon's Land at all, or knew anything about the Fairie Countries of the Western World."

"When you left there, you came straight to this town of Haubeck?" asked Hinzelmann.

"Yes."

"And you have lived here in the same house ever since?"

"I have lived here in the same house ever since," said Hautchen proudly.

"It is marvelous," said Hinzelmann. "I did not know any one could be so stupid. To live in this house so long and know so little about it."

He jumped off the table into the wet below.

"Hurry. Hurry. Are you going to mop the floor forever? It is little enough sport to sit and watch, I can tell you. Give me a rag and a pole that we may at last be done. You are to come to the attic with me. There is something there that I would show you."

When they reached the attic, Hinzelmann made straight for the eaves and crawled far, far in and pulled out something strange from the dark underneath them.

"Have you ever seen this before?" he asked.

"It looks like a string," said Hautchen apologetically. "No, it is not a string. It is a piece of leather. Or—no." He felt it cautiously. "It cannot be leather, for it feels like something else. I have it. It is a woman's girdle. And it is woven out of some kind of silk—or something."

Hinzelmann grunted as he picked it up.

"Let go and stand back and keep out of the way," he said. "I will show you something."

He took the girdle by one end and—

Hautchen never understood what it was that Hinzelmann did with it. Did he twitch it or snap it or throw it in the air? At any rate, the girdle—if it was a girdle—writhed and twisted and grew in wondrous wise. Great folds rose out of it and fluttered in the air and swept a sickening breeze through the attic.

Hautchen hid behind the rafters and shook with fright.

"What is this wild thing that you have picked out of the house?" he chattered.

"It is a Witch Cloak," said Hinzelmann. "And there seems to be no one to tell however it came here. If the Witches had but an inkling of its whereabouts, they would search the whole town through till they found it. I can promise you that."

He seized hold of one corner and, whether he snapped it or twisted it, Hautchen could not tell. But the cloak shrunk small again and lay as it had lain before, limp and unmoving. Hinzelmann held it out to Hautchen.

"Feel it," he said. "Is it not soft and beautiful?"

But Hautchen shrank back. It was best to be wary of things one did not know about.

"What do Witch Cloaks do?" he asked.

"They strangle people."

Hautchen caught his breath.

"They kill people, you mean?" he gasped.

"They could easily," said Hinzelmann in a very grand way. "And sometimes they really do. But the Witches are not bad at heart. Leave them alone, give them whatever they wish—and you have little trouble. I have seen them often—when I lived with my present mistress's aunt—and before that even. The Witch Maids came down from the hills to steal hempstalks from the fields. The peasants could not see them, but saw the hemp awave in their wake and tried to stop the pillage. Then, out came the Witch Cloaks to choke and strangle, till the stupid men fell to the

ground or ran away—and the Witch Maids cut their
spoil in peace and furled their cloaks and made off.
And the stupid peasants stayed behind, gasping for
hours afterwards. But what ails you, Spindle Legs?
Tears? Tears? Do you weep for the peasants or the
Witch Maids? Or what?"

"I weep for myself," sobbed Hautchen. "Oh, that
dreadful woman! Oh, that cloak! Why did I not
know? Why did I not know?" And Hautchen rocked
to and fro on the attic floor.

"What are you talking about?" asked Hinzelmann
in amaze. "What woman is it that you want to know
about?"

"Oh, the New Baker's Fat Wife. But, oh, I do not
want to know about her. Not I. Not ever."

And he told Hinzelmann of that awful woman
and the time he had had with her and the many things
she did not do and of the few things which she did do
—all of which she should have let alone. And at last
—in a whisper—he told Hinzelmann of how he had
got rid of her.

"And the sad part of it is," said Hautchen, as he
wiped his eyes, "that if I had only known, I could
have used this Witch Cloak upon her—and—and, oh,

my troubles would have come to an end long before they did."

Hautchen began to cry again. But Hinzelmann laughed uproariously. Hinzelmann had listened with a joyous smile to the tale of the bread flying at the heads of the New Baker's customers, and now he slapped Hautchen on the back and called him a fine fellow.

"You are a man after my own heart," said Hinzelmann. "I did not know that you had so much spirit in you. You are a finer fellow than I ever dreamed of. Let us take the Witch Cloak and go down into the streets of Haubeck and enjoy ourselves."

Like two bad little boys they slipped along the streets, looking for something to catch with the Witch Cloak. Hinzelmann was for letting fly at any or every man who came along. But the courage began to ooze out of Hautchen's shoes, and when two of the Town Fathers came strutting along home from an evening meeting he fairly began to shake, for Hinzelmann's one thought was to let the Witch Cloak loose on the two portly gentlemen and see what would happen.

"You cannot do that. You cannot do that," Hautchen cried out under his breath. And he gripped Hinzelmann's arm and would not let go until the two important persons were well past. "What do you suppose would become of us, if the Goblins were to hear of such an outrage? Why, they would be ready to throw us out of Haubeck. Let us go and chase cats. We can harm no one if we chase cats."

So they went to chase cats. They crawled along the tops of high walls. They scrambled over steep roofs. They hid in dark corners. They found cats and cats and cats. And they let fly the Witch Cloak and watched the wild rolling about and heard the wilder spitting. And they were as happy as ever were any two Goblins in the little town of Haubeck.

After a while Hinzelmann tired of cats. They were tearing great holes in the cloak, he declared; and he would none of them.

"Besides, they are not the sport that mortals are. Let us go find us a man."

But Hautchen shook his head.

"The Goblins of Haubeck—you do not know what a terrible lot they are," he said. "They love the mortals. What would happen to us if they heard that we had been having a sport with the people of Haubeck, I do not dare even to think of. Let us go instead to the pump in the Market Place. It is built to look like a man and when you pump, the water comes out of the mouth. We will go and send the Witch Cloak after the pump. The Cloak will be none the wiser. It will think the pump is a man indeed—and every one will be as well satisfied."

"All right," Hinzelmann agreed good-naturedly.

But there was a twinkle in his eye as he spoke, and he kept a sharp lookout to right and left.

Just as they were turning into the Market Place they came full upon a party of serenaders, five or six young men who had nothing better to do o' nights than to hang guitars around their necks by ribbons and go about the town, singing songs under pretty girls' windows.

Hautchen pulled Hinzelmann back sharply against the wall. What was the use of bumping into them, when they could not see you and would be sure to grow much excited and talk about ghosts or at least great armies of men who were about to climb over the walls and kill everybody in Haubeck?

Hinzelmann said not a word, as Hautchen pulled him back. But the arm that held the shrunken Witch Cloak wriggled strangely. And the next thing the

. . . arms and legs waving wildly.

Goblin knew that Cloak was sailing away through the air and had lit on the heads of the gay serenaders.

Now it so happened that some forty of the belfry Goblins had been taken with the wish to go and dance in the Town Hall that night; and at the moment when the Cloak and the young men became entangled at the corner, they turned into the Market Place from another little street close by.

Hautchen saw them. They saw the confusion— arms and legs waving wildly, a great, black flapping something overhead—and they heard many angry words. Hautchen rushed forward to pull the Witch Cloak off of the young Haubeckers; and then the Goblins saw Hautchen. But Hautchen was not practiced in the art of casting and furling Witch Cloaks and in a trice he also was mixed up with the Cloak and the singers, the ribbons and guitars.

The belfry Goblins surged forward to see what all this uproar was about. But the outcry was bringing the good people of Haubeck to door and window, and men were already rushing to the rescue of their fellows.

The belfry Goblins decided with one accord that the ground was no safe resting place and took to the

little balconies that lined the sides of the houses. And
Hinzelmann, afraid that through some mischance
water might be poured upon the Cloak and its magic
virtues spoilt, slipped forward, snatched the Cloak
back into his hand and made off, dragging the half-
choked Hautchen with him.

"It is no use," sighed Hautchen.

They had reached their house in safety and were
sitting close together under the eaves in the attic, their
feet tucked under them and their chins on their knees.

"It is no use. The belfry Goblins saw us. Now they
are talking the matter over. Before morning we shall
have to tell them what happened. And all the Goblins of Haubeck will be there to listen."

Even as he spoke, a pair of slim legs shot in at the
dormer window and a breathless Goblin invited them
to the Town Hall to tell what the trouble had been.
All the Goblins were waiting for them. The news had
gone like wild-fire around the little city that something had happened.

Hautchen told the story. In the big Town Hall the
Goblins listened, breathless. Hinzelmann brought out
the shrunken Witch Cloak and explained how such
things were used by the dreaded Witch Ladies. Haut-

chen declared that they had been hunting cats. House Goblins bristled up all around the Hall. Had Hautchen and Hinzelmann been hunting *their* cats, they wanted to know?

Hautchen made haste to assure them that they had not. He and Hinzelmann had been hunting the cats that belonged to nobody and were wont to hurt the house cats of Haubeck. The House Goblins settled down again, and Hautchen went on to explain that the Cloak had jumped out of Hinzelmann's hand by accident, when he pulled Hinzelmann out of the way to keep him from bumping the serenaders and frightening them.

And Hinzelmann stood by and looked solemn and said never a word.

Now, if the truth of the matter were told, there was not a Goblin in all that Hall who would not have been more than glad to have chased cats—or anything else—through the streets of Haubeck with Hautchen and Hinzelmann and the Witch Cloak. But do you think they were going to tell any one that? Not they.

They looked wise and they shook their heads and they said that it would not do. Of course, it had been an accident—they understood that. But the accident had showed plainly that it was not safe to have any such a thing as a Witch Cloak in Haubeck. Here the whole city had been wrought up because of it. The Witch Cloak must be burnt.

And they all piled out of the Town Hall to see that it was done.

Hautchen was very discouraged. He did not like to be mixed up in things that were unpleasant. Although that time was past when no one spoke to him because of his ungoblinlike behavior in the matter of the milk pans in the Baker's house and the flowers that flew at the Miller's head—still, he had not forgotten it. And he did not care for any such times to return.

Hinzelmann on the other hand was quite cheerful as the two walked home together through the streets at dawn. The burning of the Witch Cloak seemed to have bothered him but little. And nothing else bothered him at all.

"Why are you so downhearted?" he asked Hautchen. "No one grumbled at you, or said that the fault was yours."

"That is true," Hautchen agreed; and he brightened up at once. "But, Hinzelmann," he said after a while, "how strange that Witch Cloak looked as it

was being burnt. Not at all as it looked in the attic,
or later, on the streets. It looked more like a piece of
rope than anything else. Did it not seem so to you?"

Hinzelmann considered.

Then, "So it did," he agreed solemnly. "So it did."

He turned and winked at the rising sun; for the
Witch Cloak had not been burnt at all—Hinzelmann
had seen to that. It was only a piece of rope that had
been burnt after all.

THE UNBIDDEN GUEST

The UNBIDDEN GUEST

ALL THE GOBLINS OF HAUBECK were huddled together in Lurin's belfry.

Midwinter was past and the many naps and yawns that went with it. Patches of snow still dotted the ground and the north wind blew chill. But from time to time there was a feeling in the air that said, "Spring is coming back again."

And so the Goblins were already planning their summer doings.

While they were chattering, there came flying leaps on the belfry stairs and Rig, the Tin Smith's stay-at-home Goblin, burst in upon them.

"Come with me," he cried, "and tell me whether I have gone mad, or whether what I see is true."

He would say no more, but hurried them downstairs again, the wondering Goblins trooping at his heels.

Through the chilly little streets they went and stopped at last before the Weaver's house.

"Look in there," Rig ordered. "And tell me what you see."

The Goblins stood tiptoe to look in at the frosted windows. Then they climbed onto the window-ledge to see the better. Those behind climbed onto one another's shoulders, and the others swung up the bare grapevine that grew against the house. Some few fidgeted below, waiting their chance.

At last all climbed down again and stood shivering in the street.

"It cannot be that we are all mad," they assured one another solemnly.

"Let us find Kautz and ask him the meaning of this."

Kautz was the Weaver's Goblin; and they searched for him, high and low. But Kautz was the one person in Haubeck whom they were unable to find.

"Let us consider the matter," they said at last.

And they went back to Lurin's belfry to talk it over.

But talking did no good; and all the night through they stole out in groups of a dozen or so, to peep in at the Weaver's windows and see what new thing had happened since they last looked.

When dawn came every Goblin in Haubeck had been to the Weaver's windows—every Goblin, except Hautchen, that is.

Hautchen was so taken up with the Wood Carver's children these days that he had little time for gadding. The baby was teething and had to be amused at nights. And besides there was Hinzelmann who had to be kept in order.

"Let us go and tell Hautchen," the Goblins said at last in despair. "And if he can make nothing of it, let us get him to ask Hinzelmann. Hinzelmann is a crusty fellow—he cares for nothing and nobody. But some-

times—does it not seem to you sometimes—that he
has a fondness for Hautchen?"

They went to the Wood Carver's house and whispered for Hautchen to come out. And when he came,
they nearly fell over one another telling him their
tale.

"Rig the Tin Smith's Goblin tipped over the yeast
last night," they said. "And he went across roofs to
borrow a setting from Kautz in the Weaver's house.
He could not find Kautz and in his search he went to
the room where the family sat about. And what do
you think he saw? An ugly little blear-eyed old man
no bigger than Liesel hopping about the room. The
Weaver and the Weaver's Wife both called the ugly
little old fellow, 'Liesel' and took him—first one and
then the other—on their knees and kissed him and
fondled him and at last put him in Liesel's bed for the
night. Have you ever heard the like, Hautchen? Tell
us that, now. Have you ever heard the like? We have
been there many times this night, and Liesel we have
not seen at all. The fellow with the nightmare face
lies in her crib, a-grinning at the ceiling. When the
Weaver people sleep, out he whisks to dance about
the room, sit atop the stove and jump over the table.

When they turn and wake, back he is in Liesel's crib with his head on her pillow. What does it mean, Hautchen? Our heads are like to split with the thinking and we cannot find the Weaver's Kautz so that we can learn how these things came to be."

Hautchen could not tell what it meant. He turned white when he thought about Liesel. She was the only child in the Weaver's house. And there was no telling what might happen to the Weaver's wife, if anything happened to her. For the Weaver's Wife was not strong—and her one thought was little Liesel.

"Let us go and get Hinzelmann and go and look," he said.

And that was what the Goblins wanted.

Hinzelmann gave one look in at the window and then climbed off the ledge, shrugging his shoulders. The rest crowded around breathless, waiting for him to speak. Hinzelmann shrugged his shoulders again as he looked at them.

"It is a Changeling," he said. "Some of the Fairie Folk have stolen Liesel and put this thing in her place, leaving a blindness upon her parents, so that they shall not know the difference. What are you going to do about it?"

The Goblins looked at one another in fright.

"Let us go and talk it over," one of them managed to gasp out at last.

And they all trooped back to the belfry in great relief.

Hautchen and Hinzelmann went back to the Wood Carver's to begin the day's work.

Late the next night the Goblins appeared again at their door. The Goblins were heated, and despair was written on their faces. Hinzelmann climbed out of the churn to listen to their tale. And Hautchen hustled them up into the attic before they could disturb the baby.

"You said he was a Changeling," they said reproachfully to Hinzelmann. "We fell upon him this night and dragged him out of the house and beat him in the Market Place. Is it not a law that when a Changeling is beaten in the Market Place, the mortal child is returned and the Changeling is whisked away by the Fairie Folk? Do you think that Liesel was brought back to us? She was not brought back. Nothing was brought back. So we have picked him up and carried him off and pitched him back into the Weaver's house. And he has crawled back into Liesel's little bed and lies there, still smirking—with his back black and blue. Hinzelmann, what *are* we to do?"

"Did you make him speak?" asked Hinzelmann.

The abashed Goblins looked at one another and shook their heads. They had not made him speak.

Hinzelmann stared at them.

"The Goblins of Haubeck," he murmured. "They are a fine lot."

And he went downstairs and crawled back into his churn. He would have nothing further to do with them, and they had to go away.

But the next evening they were back.

"Hinzelmann," they wailed, "we have tried everything. And we cannot make him speak."

Then Hinzelmann rose up in great anger. He seized the dasher of his churn and rushed out into the street. And the Goblins strung along behind him with their mouths open.

Hinzelmann was quicker than the Goblins. When they reached the Weaver's house, Hinzelmann was already within. He had this Changeling squirming on the floor and was rolling the star-shaped end of the dasher up and down the Changeling's sides. Just as the Goblins crowded up to see, the ugly little fellow on the floor broke into a number of unwilling, squeaky giggles. Whereupon Hinzelmann whipped the dasher under his arm and whipped the Changeling out of the house by the coat collar.

"You come with me," he said sternly. "We wish to have words with you."

The Goblins looked on, sighing.

"Now, why did we not think of that?" they whispered to one another. "Of course, if you make him laugh, then he must speak with you. He has no choice."

They took him to the belfries and set him in their midst and questioned him.

"I am a Changeling. Yes," he told them. "It is my business. I have followed that calling for years. Sometimes I am a wee child. I lie in a cradle and suck my thumb and cry. If the maid gives me sugar on the sly, I rise be-nights and do her work for her. If she slaps me or sticks pins into me— Well," he grinned, "she pays for it. Sometimes I am quite a large child—as now. Sometimes even a grown girl. You see, I am accomplished. And the people to whom I go never know."

"The greater idiots they," growled the Goblins.

"But what we want to know is, where is our Liesel?"

"I do not know," said the Changeling. "I have not been told."

"If we beat you long enough in the Market Place, will she be brought back to us?"

"If you beat me from now until the winter comes again, still she will not be brought back to you."

"But do you think we are such great fools?" they cried out to him. "And the Folk who sent you, do they think that we are so dull that we do not know your trick? And you and the Folk, is it in your minds that we will sit tamely by and let this thing go on? Have none of you heard of us—the Goblins of Haubeck?"

"We have," the ugly little old man laughed promptly. "We have heard of the Goblins of Haubeck many times. They are known to be the greatest chicken-hearts and the greatest simpletons in Elfdom. We do not fear you. What will you do?"

The Goblins looked at one another. The little man laughed again and went on.

"You do not know where Liesel is," he said. "You do not know where to look for her even. Even if you did, you would sit here shivering, instead of going out to search, and would tell each other how cold the earth is in wintertime and how dangerous it is to stir beyond your city walls. We know you. Now—what are you going to do about it?"

The Goblins fairly chattered with rage.

But Hinzelmann asked with elaborate politeness, "Then you think perhaps to live here forever, sitting on the knee of the Weaver's Wife and smirking up into her face?"

"Oh, no," he answered easily. "Before long I shall sicken. And then I shall die. And none of the Haubeckers will be the wiser. And then I shall go back to my own home—until I go to the mortals as a Changeling again."

The Haubeck Goblins turned white with fear. If the Changeling died, playing that he was Liesel, the Weaver's Wife would surely die of sorrow, for she was not strong and had already had much trouble.

Hinzelmann, though, turned red with rage. He seized this Changeling fellow by the coat collar and dragged him down the belfry stairs. He dragged him through the streets of Haubeck, shaking him all the while. And between the shakes he spoke his mind.

"You have seen me before," Hinzelmann said

The Goblins fairly chattered with rage.

fiercely. "And you have felt my churn dasher. Do you remember? It was five villages from here, where the old woman lived on the peasant farm and you took the place of her plowman's little boy. You know me and my ways. See to it, therefore, that you delay this death of yours until I give the word—else it will fare with you as it did that other time. Only this time it will be worse."

"But if the Folk bid me to die, what am I to do?" gasped the Changeling, trying to loosen his coat collar.

"I have said what I have said," snapped Hinzelmann, as he pitched the little fellow into the Weaver's house. "Die before I give the word, and it will fare with you as it did that other time—only it will fare worse."

And Hinzelmann went back to his own house.

Meanwhile the Goblins of Haubeck did not know what to do. Should they take this Changeling away from the Weaver's house, or should they not? They spent their days and nights in talking the matter over. And before they were well aware of it the pussy willows had burst open on the willow boughs, the swallows and violets were come and spring was abroad in the land.

And with the swallows and the spring Kautz the Weaver's Goblin suddenly appeared in Haubeck— Kautz, who had disappeared so strangely on the day when Liesel, too, had disappeared and who had not been heard from since.

Kautz was in a furious temper.

"And are you sitting here, talking and talking and doing nothing for her?" he cried, as he looked them over.

But the other Goblins grew furious too.

"Why did you not guard the child yourself?" they wanted to know. "If it is Liesel you are speaking of. You were House Goblin in her home."

Kautz stamped his foot.

"And have I spent these weary winter months searching for her in the snowy world, to come back and be told that I have failed in duty to the Weaver's house and child?" he cried. He was so angry that tears came to his eyes. "I saw the Fairie Folk steal her and make off with her and I followed, thinking to keep an eye on her and get her back again. Somehow—how, I know not— they slid themselves and the child from under my very fingers, and all trace of them was lost. Then I turned back for help and have been many days coming here—and now that I am back, what do I find? A hideous, blear-eyed little old man placed in the house as Changeling, lording it in the Weaver's family, and the Goblins sitting in their belfries hugging their knees and biting their nails over it."

The Goblins rose up on all sides to defend themselves.

"But what can we do?" they cried. "So long as the Weaver's Wife thinks him Liesel, all is well. If we take him away, she thinks the child is lost and goes mad with grief."

For answer Kautz shook his fists in the air and rushed down the belfry stairs.

"He has gone to murder the Changeling," the Goblins whispered one to another, and they scurried after to see what would happen.

But Kautz had made for the Wood Carver's house, pulled Hinzelmann, all sleepy and protesting—for it was mid-afternoon and the sun was shining brightly—out of his churn and told him the story.

"Come with me and help me," he ended breathlessly. "One could talk the year round and still those mush-head Goblins could not be made to see that it is better for the Weaver's Wife to sorrow now and search

until the real Liesel is found again, than to be happy
a little while and then sorrow forever."

"You are quite right," Hinzelmann agreed. "If the
Changeling is not allowed to play at dying before their
eyes—as he was bidden to do when he came here—
then he will surely be whisked away by the Fairie
Folk, no matter how sharp a watch is kept over him.
And then where will be the chance of getting Liesel
back again? We must take him away at once and keep
him, so that the people of Haubeck will begin to
hunt."

The two set out together, each greatly pleased with
the other. They went to the Weaver's house and they
fell upon the Changeling who was stealing jam in the
pantry and had smeared the sweet stuff all over the
shelves. They bound him and took him away across
roofs to the Wood Carver's house and dumped him in
at the attic window. And all the while he smirked and
giggled and asked what other clever idea had come to
them and what did they think they were going to do
with him now?

And the belfry Goblins followed from afar and
looked on and did not dare to say anything.

Before long there was an outcry in the street below,

that Liesel the Weaver's little daughter was lost. People began searching their cellars and chests of drawers, and the Goblins came in by twos and threes at the attic windows of the Wood Carver and told Kautz and Hinzelmann that it really would not do. The Weaver's Wife had been fainting already. The Changeling would have to be sent back to her without delay—and that was all there was to it.

Kautz and Hinzelmann sat there, one at the head, the other at the feet of the bound Changeling and answered them never a word.

The Goblins slipped away again to go to the belfries and talk it over. And Kautz and Hinzelmann sat there like stones. And the outcry in the streets grew louder. And the sun went down.

Suddenly the Changeling sat up.

"What is this that they are saying?" he gasped. "What are they saying? Undo my hands—quick—and untie my feet. What are they calling to one another down there?"

Kautz and Hinzelmann looked at one another and their jaws fell. Surely, they had not thought that the charm would work so quickly. They ran to the window to see.

In the streets below people were crying to one another, "All is well. All is well. The search is over. The Miller of Brocken found Liesel in his Mill."

When they turned back into the attic again, the Changeling had slipped his hands free and was untying his feet. In another moment he would have been gone.

The Weaver's Wife was sure that her little Liesel was coming down of a fever—the child spoke so strangely and seemed to think she had been gone so long a while and said she had seen so many strange sights. But Liesel's appetite stayed as large and healthy as ever, and after a while she stopped talking about the strange sights she had seen. So the Weaver's Wife decided after a while that she must have been mistaken.

And the Changeling?

He led a terrible life of it in the attic of the Wood Carver's house. He wanted to get away. Something had plainly gone amiss in the plans of the Fairie Folk who had sent him as Changeling to this place. But do you think that Kautz and Hinzelmann let him go?

Not they. They kept him there and kept a strict watch over him, and the Goblins came in and looked at him. And he had to do every trick he knew how to do and tell every tale he knew how to tell. And for thirteen days he led a miserable life of it.

Then Kautz decided that it was time for house-cleaning in the Weaver's home. And Hinzelmann decided that the spring sunshine was too beautiful to be missed. And they let him go.

And they heard him say, as he made for the attic stairs, "If ever I set foot in Haubeck again—"

WHAT
THE WOOD CARVER DID

WHAT THE WOOD CARVER DID

THE CHANGELING WAS THE one who really caused all the trouble that followed.

Whenever Hinzelmann thought of how he and Kautz had got the better of that dreadful little old man, it made him jump for joy. For surely the only reason that Liesel came back to Haubeck was because they had carried off the Changeling. And then the spring crept into Hinzelmann's veins. And that finished things.

The Wood Carver's children went for a walk by

themselves. And Hautchen, who feared that they might get into trouble or mischief, went along to keep an eye on them. The Wood Carver's Wife took the baby and went to drink afternoon coffee with a friend. Hinzelmann stayed at home and felt the spring winds blowing past the kitchen windows and smelt the little bunch of lilies-of-the-valley in a glass on the kitchen table.

So he climbed to the top of the stairs with the churn on his back and he rolled the churn down again with himself in the inside of it.

It was an old habit of his. In former days when he felt happy he had always rolled downstairs inside of a churn. But since he had come to Haubeck, Hautchen would not let him do it. And that was one of the chief reasons that the Wood Carver's family thought that they were rid of him.

But to-day—well, there was no one at home to know anything about it. So Hinzelmann rolled down the stairs in peace.

And the Wood Carver came in and caught him.

The Wood Carver did not usually come home so early in the afternoon. But the spring had crept into his veins too and he wanted to take a walk with his wife. And he opened the door of his house to see the family churn bumping down the stairs with Hinzelmann's delighted face at one end of it.

When the Wood Carver's Wife came home, she found her husband sitting in the middle of the room with the churn on one side of him and Hinzelmann on the other.

"Look," said the Wood Carver, pointing.

And that was all that he had to say.

When Hautchen came home later with the children, he found Hinzelmann sitting in a heap on the attic floor. And Hinzelmann told him the whole story.

"What are you going to do about it?" asked Hautchen.

Hautchen felt as though his heart had fallen down into the cellar.

Hinzelmann did not know.

"The man is very angry," Hinzelmann said in a small voice. "But how was I to know that he would be coming home? If I had not rolled downstairs in the churn, I should have surely burst. It is a feeling that comes over me every spring."

Hautchen shook his head sadly and went to sit be-

hind the stove in order to learn what the Wood Carver
was going to do about it.

The Wood Carver did not say. His face was white
and he shook his fist a good deal. But all he said was,
"I will not go away. And I will not stand it. He shall
see."

The next morning a large sign swung to and fro beside the front door of the Wood Carver's house. And
everybody who went by stopped with open mouth to
read it.

"House Kobold for Sale," was what the sign said.
And this was after all stupid. For Hinzelmann was
not a Kobold at all. But the people of Haubeck did
not know that.

They all flocked in to see what a House Kobold was
and to ask questions and gape about. And the Wood
Carver's face was like stone when he talked to
them.

"Our House Kobold?" the Wood Carver would say.
"He is an heirloom in my wife's family. Yes; they are
a great rarity. Few families can boast of having one.
It is no doubt a great honor. Why do we wish to part
with him? Oh, we are people of simple tastes. Also,
this house is not so large as it might be. We feel

They were ready enough to come and look at the queer little fellow.

cramped for room. That is the reason we are not asking so much money as he well might bring."

And then Hinzelmann would be brought out to be looked over.

The Goblins were aghast. What manner of doings were these? Since when had it come about that Elfin Folk could be brought out and looked over and bought and sold by mortal kind? They went to Hinzelmann in great crowds and told him not to come into sight when the Wood Carver called. He could do that easily enough—for how could the Wood Carver find him, if he did not wish to be found?

But Hinzelmann shook his head.

"You do not understand," he said with a great sigh. "My father sold me to the mortals when I was a child. And that changes everything. If it were simply work to do for them, that is one thing. Then I could hide— or do it badly. But when it is a matter of selling—ah, then I cannot help myself. Then they must have their way."

But it would seem as though people were not so eager to buy this House Kobold which the Wood Carver wished to dispose of. They were ready enough to come and talk and look at the queer little fellow, who came forth unwillingly enough when he was called and stood before them. But as to buying—

"Why, what should we do with him?" they asked with a shrug of the shoulder.

"You might put him on the chimney piece as an ornament," the Wood Carver answered grimly.

Then the people would laugh and say that the Wood Carver was a wit and turn and go back to their homes. And the Wood Carver would be left with his House Kobold on his hands.

The Goblins took heart again. Maybe Hinzelmann would go on living in the Wood Carver's house, because he could not be got rid of. They had grown almost fond of Hinzelmann. As for Hautchen, he brightened up wonderfully at the prospect.

But one fine day the Wood Carver dragged out a curious old chest from under the eaves of the attic and came bumping downstairs with it. And he ordered Hinzelmann to get into it. And he hired another man to help him carry his burden to the Market Place.

There he took his stand and began crying his wares along with the other people, who were calling out that they had fresh vegetables and pots and coats and shoes and what-not for sale.

"A House Kobold here," called the Wood Carver. "To be given away with this beautiful old carved chest. No House Kobold; no chest. The two go together."

For you must know that a House Kobold or Goblin—or be his name what it may be—cannot be given away secretly. The new owner must know what he is getting and be willing to accept it—else the Kobold comes straight back to his old owner again.

For three months the Wood Carver went twice every week to the Market Place and offered his chest and Kobold to every passer-by—the country people who came to Haubeck on the Market days to sell and buy, as has been the custom of the land since any one can remember. And then at last one morning there came a tall, stern old man walking through the Market Place.

He stopped and listened to the Wood Carver, whose voice was nearly gone from much shouting. He looked at the chest. And he looked at the unhappy little Hinzelmann. And he said that he would take the two.

Before the dazed Wood Carver knew what had happened, a wagon had driven up to his side, two men had lifted chest and Kobold into it, the stern old man had mounted in front, and they all had gone clatter-ing off down the street towards the City Gate.

Hautchen, who had grown so worked up over the Wood Carver's doings that he could no longer rest at home, saw the whole thing and ran sobbing to the belfries to tell the Goblins what had happened.

THE CABBAGE PATCH

THE CABBAGE PATCH

THE CABBAGE PATCH WAS A beautiful place. It stretched out on all sides like a park. Little streams of water ran here and there through the middle of it and tiny paths wound among the cabbages. A huge stone wall shut it in on all sides and a deep ditch surrounded the wall on the outside. So it looked as though outsiders were not wanted in the Cabbage Patch.

Hautchen sat on the top of the stone wall—he was looking for Hinzelmann; he had run away from Haubeck and had been looking for Hinzelmann for months—and peered down into the Cabbage Patch.

He had never seen such cabbages in his life—so large and beautiful. They looked as though they had been frosted and they glimmered, some deeply purple, some pearly green in the light of the summer moon.

Hautchen was dripping wet from his passage through the big ditch on the outside of the great wall. How he had come alive from out of all that water he hardly knew. And how he had managed to climb that wall he did not know at all.

"And now I must get me down into this place," he sighed, as he made ready to drop. "Who knows what the end of this will be?"

He dropped and rolled under some of the cabbages. For strange animals were abroad in the place and he did not care for more adventures. He had had enough of them since he had left Haubeck.

The animals looked enormous. They had long necks and long legs and they stalked solemnly about in the moonlight, cocking their heads and looking at the cabbages as they passed.

Hautchen looked at the cabbages too, as he lay among them. They seemed to be stirring ever so slightly on their stalks. There were soft little sounds down here close to the ground where they grew, sounds that might be the beginning of murmured songs or tiny bursts of laughter or a soft mingling of the two.

Hautchen listened. He could not make it out at all. A moment later he forgot all about it, for there came another something along the path near which he lay. This new something crouched and slid from shadow to shadow behind those other long-legged animals. Hautchen looked and looked. His heart came up into his throat. He wriggled forward. Of course, he might be mistaken. One could never be sure of things in the moonlight; but—but—

"Hinzelmann," he called softly. "Hinzelmann—"

And—as sure as those cabbages were softly swaying to and fro in the moonlight—Hinzelmann tumbled out of the little path and into Hautchen's arms.

Hautchen was so excited that he was sure that he would not be able to talk at all. But, whether he knew it or not, he talked a great deal.

"Hinzelmann," he whispered. His arms were tight about Hinzelmann and Hinzelmann was crying. "Hinzelmann," whispered Hautchen, "I found the Witch Cloak which you had hid again deep under the eaves in the attic of the Wood Carver's house and had told no one about— How did you ever manage to get something that looked so much like the Cloak and have it burnt up by the Goblins in place of the true one? Well, 'tis no matter— As I said, I found the Cloak and I went with it a long journey to the land of the Witches. I went to the Witches—first, hiding the Cloak so that no one could ever again find it without my help—and I told them of the thing of theirs which I had and was willing to part with—if I got what I wanted for it.

"They were most eager to have it back again—the thing must indeed be of great value to them—and they gave me much gold and besides that they gave me a thing which has so far been of much more worth than all the gold to me—a little stick with leaden nobs at the end of it. See. This. They put some magic upon it and swore that, if I only followed where it pointed, it would surely bring me in time to you. A pretty dance it has led me."

Hautchen shivered in his wet clothes.

"But since the word is kept and it has in truth pointed the road that leads to Hinzelmann, then all is well. Now with the gold we have got us for the Cloak we will buy you free. And then we will go where we will and do what we please— But however did you get into such a place as this Cabbage Patch?"

"The old man who bought me from the Wood Carver brought me here," sighed Hinzelmann.

He kept tight hold of Hautchen. It was almost as though he feared that Hautchen might run away.

"And do you cut the cabbages for the old man?" asked Hautchen wonderingly.

Hinzelmann laughed at the question.

"Cut cabbages? Not I. These cabbages are never cut. Can you not see that they differ from the cabbages that are grown in the peasants' gardens? Who ever heard of cabbages that sway to and fro and croon to themselves in the moonlight? These cabbages are the homes of little children, until such a time as they are taken by the storks to the homes of the mortals. And the old man keeps me here to exercise the storks."

Hautchen listened with his mouth open. He did not understand very well. So Hinzelmann had to explain further.

"The storks carry the children to their new homes in the lands of the mortals," said Hinzelmann. "But it is not every day that children leave the cabbages.

Then the storks have nothing to do; and, if they had no exercise to keep them strong, they might grow so weak that they would not be able to carry the children when the time came—for the journey is often long. So the old man has me ride upon the storks every day. All day long I ride them up and down the paths between the cabbages, and he stands by to see."

"H'm," said Hautchen, peering out from his hiding place at them. "So these are storks. They are larger than the ones that sometimes build their nests upon the chimney-tops at Haubeck. What were you running after them for when I called you?"

"I was trying to catch one," Hinzelmann confessed. "If I could only mount one in the night-time when the old man does not stand by to see, it might be that the stork would mount the air with me and carry me away over the wall to the country beyond. Then I could have a small season of pleasure—even though I have to come back again. For come back I must, since I have been bought and sold and given away and do not belong to myself."

"That time is past," said Hautchen gleefully. The moonlight was fading into gray. The morning was near. "That time is past. I take my gold and go

Hinzelmann had to ride up and down.

to the old man and buy you free. And then—ah, you will see how happy you will be. Life looks very different when one belongs to one's self."

Hautchen trotted off to the old man's house. Hinzelmann stayed behind and waited. His heart bobbed up and down inside of him and acted so strangely that it made his legs feel queer and he had to sit down.

He waited and waited. But Hautchen did not come back. And the sun rose and the storks gathered among the cabbages and the old man came out of his house. And Hinzelmann had to ride up and down, up and down all day long, as he had to every day on the storks, so as to give them the exercise they needed.

Hinzelmann had a lump in his throat. It seemed to him that he had never been more unhappy in his life. He did not know what had become of Hautchen and he did not dare to ask. He was strangely afraid of this old man who had the storks and the cabbages in his care.

When night came again and the moon was bright, Hautchen was again seen on the tall stone wall that surrounded the Cabbage Patch. Again he dropped down and rolled under the cabbages. And Hinzelmann rolled in on top of Hautchen.

"I thought the old man had killed you," he stammered.

Hautchen was in a rage.

"This is what comes of being polite and having kind feelings," he hissed.

He breathed hard and pounded the earth with his fists.

"I went in there to that old man. I told him our tale. I said that I had brought gold and would buy you free, because I could not be content without you. Do you think that he would listen to me? He opened a door in the wall and threw me out of the Cabbage Patch. He said that I was to come back no more, that this Hinzelmann who had been given to him was a blessing—Hinzelmann, what has come over you that you have suddenly grown into any one's blessing?— that you were not the least trouble in and about the house and that he could not possibly get along without you. Hinzelmann, what change is this? How comes it that you are no longer a trouble to the one to whom you belong?"

Hinzelmann looked terribly ashamed of himself. He tried to explain, to say that he had seen Hautchen's ways in the family of the Wood Carver, that he had thought that it might perhaps be a better plan for him to act a little more as Hautchen did. But his explanations came to nothing. He could not say anything at all and Hautchen continued to grumble.

"You have no business to be mending your ways," said Hautchen. "See now all the trouble you have put me to. If you had acted as you are wont to do, there would have been no trouble at all now. The old man would have been only too glad to be rid of you. I should have paid the gold. And by now we would be far away from here. Who knows now how long it will take before we can leave?"

Then Hautchen unfolded his plan.

It may have been an hour later that the old man who had charge of the Cabbage Patch heard a mighty knock on his door.

He opened it to find a little fellow standing on the step and looking up at him. The little fellow wore a great, wild beard over most of his face, and a wide hat was pulled down over his eyes. His eyes gleamed fiercely. His hands were clenched. And he carried a great stick.

"Can it be true," he asked in a deep voice, "that I have at last tracked a villain called Hinzelmann to the spot where he lives?"

The old man looked surprised.

"I have a Goblin called Hinzelmann," he said slowly. "But he is no villain. Why, only last night a friend of his was here, saying that life could no longer be lived without Hinzelmann and offering me gold to give him up."

The newcomer struck his staff upon the ground.

"Do not give Hinzelmann up," he cried wildly. "No matter what happens, do not give him up. It is better that you should suffer. It is better that your house should be burnt over your head—Hinzelmann will do that some day. I know him. He is but biding his time—better that your house should be burnt and you should be hurt or killed than that Hinzelmann should be allowed loose on the earth. Do not let the friend who came for him have him. That friend is no better than he. You keep Hinzelmann here under your nose. So long as he is here, the rest of us are safe. Of course, it may be unpleasant for you—but then you are a large man and will not care."

You can guess what the old man's feelings were

when he heard all this. He asked the strange little fellow in. And the stranger told hair-raising tales of Hinzelmann's doings—how he put poison in the food; how he burnt the roof over one's head and smothered one in one's bed so soon as he had made people think that he was a fine fellow and they had begun to trust him.

"I had come with chains to take him away and put him underground," the stranger finished. And sure enough he showed some chains dangling at his belt. "My comrades are waiting in the wood to help me. But so long as he is really safe here and cannot get away and you do not give him up, there is no danger for us. And after all, it may not be so bad as I have said. He may serve you for some months before the trouble with him begins."

The old man strode to the door and in an awful voice he called for Hinzelmann.

Hinzelmann came in, all wonder-eyed and quiet. But no sooner did he catch sight of the stranger than he fell to the floor.

"Do not take me away," he cried wildly. "Do not take me away. What harm will it do to you, if I stay here? It will not be *your* house that will be burnt to the ground. Your garden will not be trampled. And you will not be smothered in your bed. Let me stay here."

The old man jerked him to his feet and handed him over to the stranger.

"Take him," he said. "Put chains on him and drag him away. I want no more of him."

The stranger snapped the chains on Hinzelmann. He laid a gold piece on the table.

"That is to pay for him," the stranger said. And then in a deep voice he said to Hinzelmann, "You come with me."

And he dragged the shrieking Hinzelmann out of the door.

The old man opened the gate for them and shoved them on to a kind of little drawbridge that stretched from there across the big ditch, and slammed the gate shut after them.

They were left on the other side—safe.

They ran, ran, ran to the nearest woods, and once there Hautchen pulled off the hat, the beard and the cloak. And he took the chains from Hinzelmann's wrists.

"We must set that scarecrow I borrowed these

clothes from to rights again, Hinzelmann," he said. "And then we must wait for the morning. I want to go back and give that old man some more money. You are worth more than one piece of gold. I think too that I shall tell him what we have done. You are free now, so he cannot get you back again. And I should feel better to have him know the truth about you— After that,"—and Hautchen's face beamed as he spoke—"why, after that, Hinzelmann, since you are free, we can do whatever we please— Would it not be nice to go back to Haubeck?"

And Hinzelmann sat down on an old tree-stump and burst into tears and sobbed that it would.

And the next day they started for the little city of Haubeck.

THE END